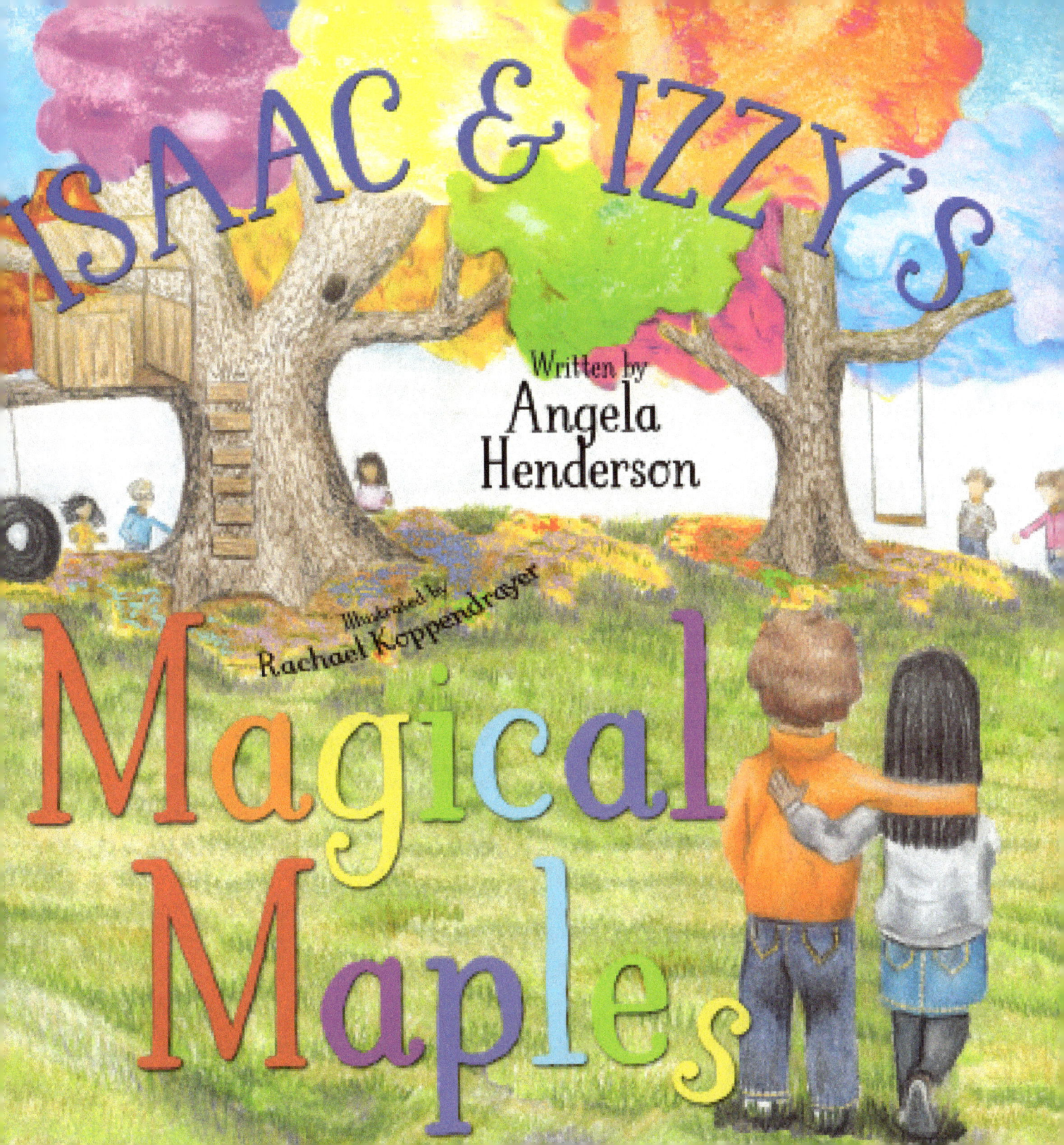

Make magical memories — with friends different & alike
Angela Henderson

ISAAC AND IZZY'S MAGICAL MAPLES

Text copyright © 2021 by Angela Henderson
Illustrations copyright © 2021 by Rachael Koppendrayer

This is a work of fiction. All characters and events portrayed in this novel are either fictitious or used fictitiously.

All rights reserved. Reproduction in part or in whole is strictly forbidden without the express written consent of the publisher, with the exception of a brief quotation for review purposes.

Cover and interior layout by Roseanna White Designs

WhiteSpark Publishing, a division of WhiteFire Publishing
13607 Bedford Rd NE / Cumberland, MD 21502
www.WhiteSpark-Publishing.com

ISBN: 978-1-941720-70-7 (paperback)
978-1-941720-72-1 (hardcover)
978-1-941720-71-4 (digital)

As Longfellow wrote,
"Into each life some rain must fall…"

I am thankful for all of my friends,
different and alike, that jump into the
"leaf piles" of life, stick with me
in the storms, and run after the rainbows—
especially my mother, Judy Primo,
who became my best friend.
After eleven years of her absence,
her seeds of love and friendship
still continue to bloom.

Autumn blew in with its crisp, cool air.
Isaac and Izzy sat in their Sugar Maple tree
munching on their favorite fall treats—
pumpkin seeds, crunchy apples, and candy corn.

The creatures were bustling around them,
eating treats of their own, and preparing for
colder days ahead. Mr. and Mrs. Blue Jay gathered
berries while Mr. Squirrel stashed away acorns.
Rabbit ransacked the shed to insulate his burrow,
and Porcupine poked around looking busy.

No matter what, they all stuck together.

Isaac and Izzy noticed that their Sugar Maple did not have any trees nearby. They wondered if maybe he needed a tree friend.

"Do you want a friend like you?" Isaac asked his tree.

Sugar Maple shook up and down, tingling from limb to limb.

At that moment, Isaac knew they were in for another
adventure with their Sugar Maple,
but this time Isaac and Izzy
would *give* their tree a surprise.

"Izzy, what if we plant a rainbow around him
and see what grows?
After all, rainbows seem to be magical
with our Sugar Maple.
I bet he'll have a tree friend grow before we know it!

"How do you plant a rainbow?" Izzy asked, puzzled.

"Follow me!" And off they ran to Isaac's house
to gather supplies.

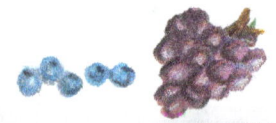

Before long, they came running back with a shovel, a bag of compost, and a rainbow of fruits—

red strawberries, orangey oranges, yellow bananas, green limes, blue blueberries, indigo plums, and purple grapes!

Isaac & Izzy planted the fruits all around the tree, digging holes with the help of some little paws and claws.

"I'm sure that something tree-like will grow from planting all these fruits," Isaac said confidently.

You'll have a friend like you before you know it!"

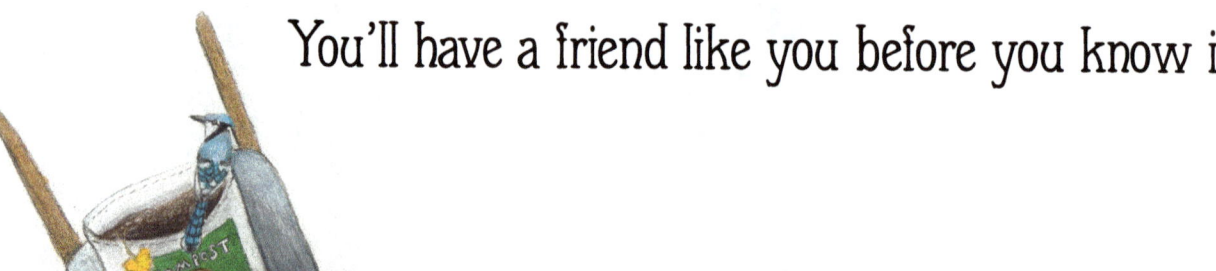

As the autumn days turned colder,
Isaac and Izzy kept their friend company.
But no sprouts from their fruits appeared.

They were starting to lose hope
for any magical moments until...

...their Sugar Maple surprised *them*.

Izzy was having a hard time believing her eyes.

"Our Sugar Maple gave us a rainbow!" she said.

Isaac grinned. "He's good at giving back."

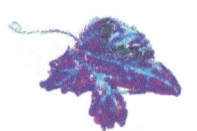

...and he gave back just in time.
That night the wind blew in harder and faster than a hurricane.

all through the neighborhood.
And as the leaves came down,
so did the Sugar Maple's seeds.

When the sun broke through the darkness,
the creatures saw fan-like-little-somethings falling from their friend.

"What are these?" Squirrel asked,
nibbling away at one.

"Hmm, maybe they are little
boomerangs?" Rabbit said,
tossing one in the air and
jumping around like a kangaroo.

"They are plummeting right down on my prickles!" complained Porcupine.

"Well, they are perfect for our nests!" exclaimed the Blue Jays.

"Wait!" hollered Fox,
rushing over to the ruckus to investigate closer.
"These are seeds! Real Sugar Maple seeds
falling from our friend!" explained Fox.
"You don't call me Fix-It-Up-Fox for nothing!
If you want your friend to have a friend like him,
we need to plant these seeds!"

Once again, they put their paws and claws together to plant the Sugar Maple's seeds in the cold, damp dirt.

Isaac woke to the sounds of the morning wind still howling.
He saw their tire swing blowing on its branch.
He smelled smashed, rotting pumpkins
rolling in from the storm.

He grabbed his raincoat and boots
and rushed to his tree,
hoping that their friend
and tree house
were not hurt.

The Sugar Maple's branches were bare,
and he was *still* the only tree in the yard.

"I'm so glad you are okay. But I'm sorry that you didn't have a friend to stand with you in the storm," Isaac said tearfully to his tree.

Just then, Isaac's tear touched the heart of a Sugar Maple seed
in the ground next to Rabbit's paw.
Before he could blink, a tiny sprout appeared.

"Isaac, look. Something is growing!" Izzy said, full of hope.

"Yes! It is!" Isaac's teary eyes grew bigger.
"And I think it may be more than just a sprout!"
Isaac pointed at the rainbow whirlwind forming
around the growth poking out of the ground.

"WOW!" Isaac and Izzy stared in wonder.
"It's impossible! How can a Sugar Maple grow up that fast?"

"Nothing is impossible with our magical Sugar Maple friend," Izzy reminded him. "Plus, it looks like we had little help...again." Izzy smiled at the creatures.
The Sugar Maple wrapped his arms around his friends—all of them—and invited the neighbors to join the fun.

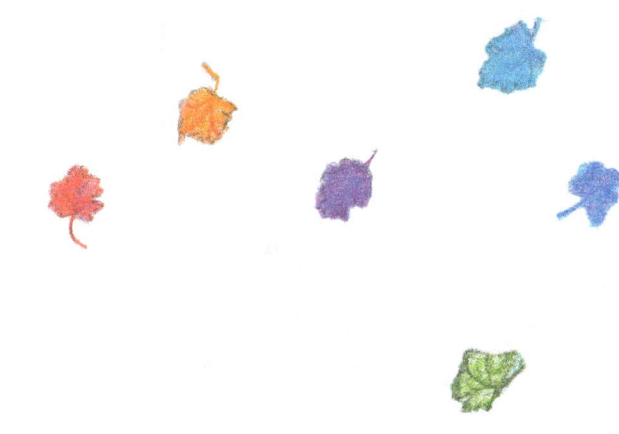

Isaac and Izzy reached their favorite spot on their favorite tree
and smiled at the two magical Sugar Maple trees standing together...
surrounded by the kids and creatures all enjoying each other
on this fine fall day.

Friends can be different or alike—
But when the stormy winds blow,
We stick together and grow.

Judy Primo's Favorite Fall Recipe

We hope that your family and friends enjoy my mom's best fall recipe! My childhood neighbors on Sunnybrook Drive certainly did as Mom and I delivered warm bread to their door and stayed a while to visit. Now my kids carry on our pumpkin bread tradition here in Sunnyvale, Texas.

Wherever you are, may your baking bring sunny days and new friendships.

Primo's Pumpkin Bread

Here's what's cookin': Pumpkin bread
Recipe from: Judy Primo   Serves: 3 loaves

- 3½ cups flour
- 3 cups sugar
- 1 cup oil
- 4 eggs
- ½ teaspoon salt
- 2 teaspoon soda
- 1 teaspoon cinnamon
- 1 teaspoon nutmeg
- 1 cup nuts
- ⅔ cup water
- 2 cups pumpkin
- 1 tea. vanilla

350° 1 hour

Mom & me

CPSIA information can be obtained
at www.ICGtesting.com
Printed in the USA
LVHW062126011021
699281LV00003B/4